Chinwag's tale

Written by Simon Frank
Illustrated by Margit Mulder

ISBN 9780992980634

iamsquarehead.com

Chinwag's tale

This is Chinwag.

He's called that because people like talking to him. He's a good listener and never barks when you're in the middle of something important.

He lives with his friend Squarehead, just over the-hill-after-next, in a little place called Squaretown.

People there have strict ideas about how things should be, especially when it comes to dogs. They say things like:

"You can't do this, you're just a dog." or

As far as they're concerned, dogs chew bones, chase balls and go for walks...and that's it.

A lot of Squaretown dogs are happy doing that, but Chinwag isn't that sort of dog.

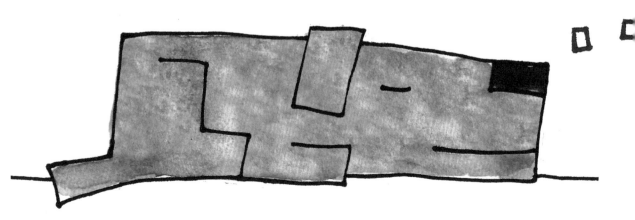

He's a dog with dreams.

For instance, the other day, he was walking past Squaretown swimming pool and thinking how lovely the water looked.

He imagined himself diving in and swimming
breaststroke, crawl, butterfly and backstroke.
He was just walking in when...

The children all laughed and poor Chinwag's little tail drooped down and he slunk off, feeling rather foolish.

Another day, he wandered into
Squaretown skateboard park.
As he watched the skateboarders,

he imagined himself kick-flipping and rail-sliding
and carving and back-siding and heel-flipping
and hippy-jumping all over the park.

"Dogs can't skateboard!"

said the attendant.

"Clear off!"

Poor Chinwag. His tail drooped even further and he crept away feeling awful.

The week after that, the circus came to town and Squarehead took Chinwag and the Hairy Scary to watch.

Chinwag imagined
himself up there in
the spotlight, with the
crowd cheering, as
he scampered along
the high wire and
flipped into a double
backwards somersault.

And he threw a bucket of water all over
Chinwag and the crowd roared with laughter.

Poor Chinwag.

Other dogs began to hear about Chinwag.
They also heard their owners saying:

"Silly dog." and...

"Dogs should know their place!" and...

Whenever a Squaretown dog passed Chinwag, he would wag his tail as if to say:

"Don't be sad! Every dog has its day."

Then, one day, an astronaut came to Squaretown and the Mayor held a big ceremony and gave him a medal for going to the moon. Chinwag wagged his tail as if to say:

"I wish I could do that."

The Mayor looked down at him and sneered.

"Dogs can't go to the moon!"

Well, I bet you can't gu

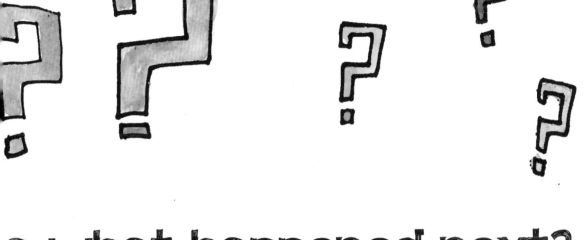

s what happened next?

Chinwag wagged his tail in a way that sent a message round to all the other dogs in Squaretown.

Over the next few weeks each of them found something to borrow from their owners that could be used to make a rocket.

There were bits of old washing machines, an old computer, a wire from a toaster, a swivel chair, an old umbrella, all sorts of little bits and pieces.

They took it all to an old garage at the end of Squaretown that nobody used.

Chinwag was too busy to go for walks any more.
He was too busy for bones and balls.
He was too busy even to stop and chat.

The day came when the rocket was ready.
The dogs towed it out into the open.
Chinwag climbed into the command module.

And then 5...4...3...2...1...

BLAST OFF!!!!!

Up and up it ZOOMED.
Higher
and higher and
higher,

until it was just a tiny speck.

And then it disappeared altogether.

It takes quite a long time for a homemade,
dog-controlled rocket to reach the moon.
But when it finally did, Chinwag jumped out,
ran around the craters, turned somersaults
and waved and barked as

loudly

as he could.

Luckily, dogs have exceptionally good hearing and all the Squaretown dogs knew that he'd got there.

That night, when their owners were asleep, all the Squaretown dogs went out into their gardens and HOWLED with delight at the moon. They howled

"WELL DONE" to Chinwag.

And they howled to each other that:

"Every dog has its day."

It was PANDEMONIUM!

It woke up babies and children and parents.

THE HOWLING WAS SO LOUD

that the Mayor of Squaretown fell out of bed
with a great big BUMP!

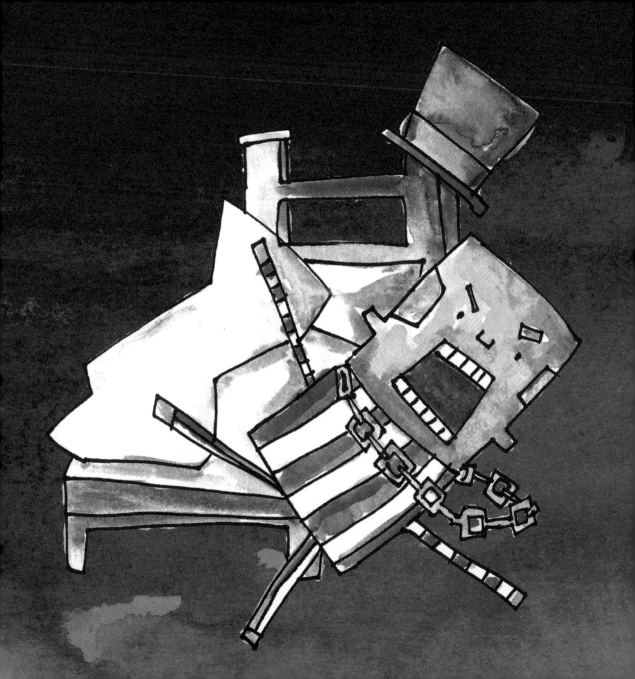

Fortunately for Chinwag, coming back to Earth was a lot quicker. (Well, it was down all the way.)

When he saw Squarehead's back garden below him, he opened his old umbrella and floated the last few feet, landing softly on the tummy of the Hairy Scary, who was having his mid-morning snooze.

Squarehead came running out of the house and gave him a big hug.

"I've missed **you!**

Where have you been?"

Chinwag wagged his tail as if to say:

"It's a long story."

No-one, not even Squarehead, ever guessed why the Squaretown dogs made such a racket that night. But you know, don't you?

And I bet you also know by now, that if anyone tries to tell you that you can't do something because you're not good enough, don't pay them any attention. **Believe in yourself** and show them just how wrong they are!

For Zac Fox; Archie and Noa Alberts; Ollie
and Dillon Kohn; Sam, Joe, Erin, & Dan Frank; Sophie;
the Mulder family; Romany & Ellis; Moses &
Daniel Barber; Dom; Vicki; Deborah; Diala and Teo.
And, of course, 3 dogs Luna, Pippa and Ziggy.

Always believe in yourself!

I am Squarehead
Written by Simon Frank   Illustrated by Margit Mulder

Hairy Scary's bad day
Another Squarehead story, written by Simon Frank, Illustrated by Margit Mulder

Get more Squarehead stories from:
www.iamsquarehead.com